Publishing history

First Edition February 2013
Email: jediaustin@hotmail.co.uk

Edited By Lisa Warburton

www.isisstockport.co.uk

ISBN 978-1-291-09313-1

Narrator – *This play centres around two people called Roger and Eunice. Both are single and unattached, they have never been married, but now they have reached 40 they feel a desperate need to find the love of their lives, which has always been missing.*

This all takes place in the town of Manchester in the year of 1994, Roger is employed as a toilet attendant in the centre of town called Piccadilly and Eunice is employed as a wig makers assistant several miles from the town centre in a place called Stretford.

Although they have visited at one time or another most of the same haunts and venues of this great northern city, they have never been aware of each other's existence but all that is soon to change as the story unfolds.

For the purpose of a better understanding of things I feel it is important to describe their appearances and a little bit of their personalities.

Roger is 5 feet 5 inches tall and weighs in at around 13 stone carrying a prominent paunch around the mid-riff. His hair or what's left of it, is raked over the top of his visibly bare scalp in the manner of Bobby Charlton in his hey-day as a football player. Roger's dress sense is shabby to say the least, perhaps dull and ill-fitted is the kindest way to describe it. An average weekly wage for Roger is in the region of £98 a week, which is spent mostly in tacky boozers and the upkeep of his one bedroom bedsit in Whalley Range.

Food is mostly of the take away variety, consisting of fish and chips, kebabs and such like.

It's been years since Roger had a girlfriend whom he had met at the local drop out centre for the rehabilitation of mentally disturbed women. But alas that ended when she left him for a 70 year old lesbian who had once been a man.

Eunice on the other hand was slightly more sophisticated, she was close to 6 foot tall, with long pink hair that tended to frizz and curl a lot. Her weight was usually somewhere around the 14 to 15 stone mark, her job as a wig-makers assistant brought her a weekly income of £140. Most of this was spent on food and the odd dress and blouse here and there.

She shared a two bed-roomed flat near Old Trafford with a female friend called Linda, who worked at Spinks cake shop.

This was a convenient arrangement for Eunice as it made shared bills and rent less stinging to the purse and also had the added perk of free cakes that had been left over from the day before where Linda worked.

The last time Eunice had a relationship with a man was a couple of years ago but sadly this came to nothing; as the Foreign Legion held greater appeal to him. Perhaps what made it more distressing for Eunice was the fact that this all took place on a day trip to France and after they had been eating at an expensive restaurant, he asked to be excused to visit the toilet and leaving her to settle up the bill, promptly did a runner.

She only learned of his joining the Foreign Legion, when he sent her a postcard. So she hadn't been able to trust men for years.

Now, we move on to the opening scene of the play, which sees us at Rogers place of work, the underground toilets in Piccadilly Manchester.

The time is early morning; 8am and Roger is just beginning his tea-break with his work mates Liam and Barry; the lads have been busy at it for the past couple of hours, wiping toilet seats and mopping floors.

Act One

The tea room in the underground toilets, Monday 8am!

Roger (Mancunian accent) – You two are a right pair of wankers, no wonder you didn't want to clean out cubicle six; the stench in their is enough to bring down the gates of heaven and as for that thing floating about at the bottom, it was like a massive crocodile, I'm sure the bugger had eyes; it winked at me.

Liam (Irish accent and laughing) – Sure, there's no one in the country better then you Roger, at breaking up those monsters my old son.

Barry (Cockney accent) – The way you turn them into submarines as they sink to the bottom, is pure class.

Roger – You pair of sweet-talking bastards, you must think I'm thicker than that log I've just done battle with, anyway that's my good deed done with for today. Anything else comes up like that, one of you can deal with it.

Liam – Did anyone suss what stinker dropped it?

Barry – I've got my suspicions, it's that small geezer that lets onto us every morning.

Roger (curious) – You don't mean Father Wilberts, from Saint Ambose Church do you?

Liam – To be sure, the very same one!

Roger – There's no way that came out of his arse, he's about six stone wet through.

Barry – Me and Liam have seen him go into cubicle six loads of times early in the morning and it's always the same, arrives with a red strained face, never smiles or lets onto us. Then ten minutes later BANG! The biggest splashing noise you ever heard and out he comes, smiling and saying, "Good morning chaps, at the top of his voice."

Roger (stunned) – Holy Shit!

Barry (agreeing) – Precisely!

Roger – No way, you're winding me up, there's no way a bugger like that could hatch out of a tight arse like that.... why the strain alone would kill him.

Liam – Listen Roger, the other week I was watching one of those nature programmes, that yer man presents, David something or other and it was all about snakes, and them bleeders can eat sheep whole in one go and yer know what small mouths they've got.

Roger (amazed) – What the hell are they feeding them down at the church?

Barry – To tell you the truth, I don't know, but the attendances have been dropping lately.

Liam – Right who's for a bacon butty, with fried egg and tomato on top?

Roger – Nice one Liam, are you going down to the breakfast bar?

Liam – No Barry, is I went yesterday!

Barry – Okay, no bother, what do you want to drink with it – Tennants or Carlsberg Special?

Roger – It's a bit too early for Tennants, so I'll just have a couple of Carlsberg's!

Liam – bloody'ell Roger, you're getting health conscious in yer old age, aren't yer?

Roger – Well, I've got to watch the belly doesn't get too big.

Barry – Right oh! I'll be back soon, as long as it takes a shit to float from here down to the local sewer plant.

Liam – Okay Roger, now that he's gone, I want you to spill the beans and tell me what's wrong! You've not looked well lately; what is it?

Roger – I'm alright man, there's nothing wrong.

Liam – Listen son, it's me you're talking too, we've worked together for years, I can spot the signs, yer know.

Roger – What flippin signs?

Liam – A few weeks ago you were bashing and breaking up shit stuck in the loos like no ones business, now it's taking ages, come on what's wrong?

Roger – Okay I might as well tell you, I've not been sleeping too good lately. I'm 40 years old and I've not got a regular bird. I can't understand it, I'm not a bad looking geezer, I've got a steady job. I mean, I'm not going to be made redundant while people have got peckers and back sides, am I?

Liam – stone me Roger, is that all that's worrying you. Everyone goes through a lean spell. It's like a football striker, sometimes he's on a hot streak and scoring in every game and other times he has games where he just can't score. Even Alan Shearer will have his off days.

Roger – What, five years of missing the back of the net.

Liam – Stone the crows, that's a long time our kid, never mind, something will crop up.

Roger – Aw, come off it Liam, you're alright you're married, you get it every night, even that ugly sod Barry's got a missus.

Liam – Come on think positive, what are you going to do about it?

Rodger – I'm jacking it in, I've come to the conclusion, I'm ahead of my time with women, they just aren't ready for me. No, I'm gonna concentrate on me darts and dominoes instead.

Liam – bloody hell Roger, is this the same guy that was telling me and Barry only a couple of months ago, that your greatest ambition was to work as an attendant in a woman's toilet.

Roger – Yeah well, sometimes life's ambitions are like the logs that float upon the waters of the toilet bowl; one minute they're up and next they go down.

Narrator – *During this cosy heart to heart in the tea-room a member of the public approaches to ask for some change, so that he may use one of the cubicles.*

Member of the public – Excuse me, but could you possibly change this pound for some ten pences please?

Liam – Hey you! Can't you see we're on our friggin tea-break? God, you lot get right up my nose, can't you hold in your dumping tackle for 10 minutes?

Member of the public (furious) – Well really I've never been so insulted in my life.

Roger (laughing) – Oh is that so, well matey you couldn't have been down here before, now go and take your backside and pollute some other bog house.

Member of the public (storming off) – I'll be writing to your manager about this and if I don't get any satisfaction then I'll contact my M.P.

Liam – You'll be wasting your time pal, we can refuse the right for anyone suspicious to brown our basins if we want.

Narrator – *As the man is storming off and up the stairs, coming down in the opposite direction and returning with the breakfast is Barry.*

Barry – Charming I must say, that ignorant git just nearly knocked the sarnies out my hands.

Liam – Don't worry yourself about him, lets get into our tucker and keg.

Barry – I don't think we're gonna have time too, I've just seen a couple of school coaches pull up and they look as if they're heading this way.

Roger – Oh no, I can't handle that, you know what the little brats are like, weeing all over the toilet seats and the floor.

Liam – What are you gonna do?

Roger – Leave it to me, I'm going to shut up shop.

Narrator – *Roger quickly hurries upstairs before the teacher and his 40 or 50 pupils descend into the toilets below.*

Roger – Sorry folks, we're not operational today; you'll have to try Marks & Spencers or somewhere like that.

Teacher – Listen my man, we've been on a long trip and all my kids have been drinking coke and there desperate to use these public facilities.

Roger - Oh is that so, well let me tell you that we're trying to repair a burst pipe down here and there are a dozen or so rats as big as cats running about all over the show, but don't let me stop you, go on, use the facilities if you must, see if I care.

Teacher – Eh umm, well another time maybe, boys back to the coach, we're heading for Marks and Spencers.

Narrator – Whilst all this was taking place and even as Roger was putting up an 'Out of Oder' sign and locking the entrance gates, Liam was briefing Barry on Rogers problem.

Liam – Listen Barry, that poor sod up there hasn't had a bird for 5 years, don't laugh, but he's just been telling me it's breaking his heart.

Barry – You're kidding man, he's always telling me how he cops regular; every weekend – well of all the lying spinners.

Liam – Have a heart Barry, the guys in a bad way, we're gonna have to think of something.

Barry – Eh up, keep stum about it, don't say a word that you've told me about it.

Liam – okay, quick act natural he's coming back.

Roger – That's sorted that out lads, now we can really put our feet up.

Liam – Nice one Roger, I was just saying to Barry, nice weather this time of the year.

Barry – Yes, I had a quiet Christmas, did you Roger? Even though I've got a bird, I could still be happy without one.

Liam – Oh for gods sake!

Roger – You've told him aint you' go on take the mick; you pair of no goods. It's not my fault, I'm too bleedin sensitive for today's women.

Liam – Don't be like that Roger, we're all muckers down here. We were just trying to come up with some ideas to help.

Roger – Sod off, I don't want to know! Where's me butty and me lager?

Narrator – *So for the next ten minutes, not a word was spoken whilst they ate, drank and read their morning papers. Then all of a sudden*

Barry jumped up with the newspaper close to his eyes and shouted.....

Barry – Yes! I don't believe it, this is just what you need Roger; it'll sort you out no danger.

Roger – If you're going to tell me about a rubber doll for sale or something sleazy like that, then up yours mate, you can forget all about it.

Liam – Yeah the last one he got run away from him!

Roger – shut up you, it was stolen by some pervy burglar, if you must know!

Barry – Now listen up you two, it's a lonely hearts column and it's asking for men to advertise.

Roger – Bollocks to that, they want a fortune off you first.

Barry (laughing) – That's the beauty of it Roger, it says it's for one week only, the advertisements free!

Liam – Dream on, you're pulling our plonkers!

Barry – Okay then feast your eyes on this if you don't believe me.

Roger – Well I'll be a son of a scorpion without a backside, it's true!

Barry – Alright were gonna do this proper. Liam go and get some paper and a pen from the drawer.

Roger – But I'm crap at writing letters, what am I gonna say?

Barry (reassuringly) – Don't worry, leave it to me, I'm not bad at English, I did a night course at college years ago and it's always stood me in good stead.

Liam (returning) – Here, I've got em!

Barry – Nice one, right lets see. 'I'm looking for a nice looking woman, between 16 years old and lets say 35'.

Liam – Cor yer getting prime beef there Roger!

Barry – Will yer keep your gob shut and let me continue. Okay, where was I? Yeah, I know now. Must be happy go lucky, attractive, a good sense of fun and into most things. Now lets describe you. My name is Charles.

Roger – Eh, what do you mean 'Charles'? that's a ponces name!

Barry – Listen do ya want a nice chick or what, cause believe me, if I say Roger, you're bound to end up with a dog; no offence mate, but I'll have to stretch the truth a bit, poetic license and all.

Liam – Go on Barry, it's getting good this!

Barry – Right I'll continue but don't interrupt me until the end, okay Roger.

Roger – Alright then!

Barry – I'm aged 32, built like a barn door hang on I'll just change that – athletic build, that's politer. After all we want to net a bit of class. I'm 5foot 10, don't worry about that; I've got some stack heels left over from the 1970's you can borrow.

Now let's see, what else, oh yea, I've got a flat in Chelsea and one in Manchester, just while I'm up here for business. I travel the world a lot, drive a posh car, let's say a jag and I earn a lot of money, my hair is thick and black and my eyes are gorgeous blue. I'm also a randy sod, I can't put that, better to say, I'm an energetic sporty type. That sounds about right so far.

Please write soon for a date, that will be the thrill of a life time. P.S I wouldn't say I was a stud but if I was a horse, I'd be knocking out winners. Lots of my love, coming your way, lucky darling, Charles.

Now if that doesn't bag you a tidy piece of skirt nought will!

Liam – But you haven't mentioned what his job is!

Barry – Blimey, I can't forget that, it's like jam to flies these days for all those gold diggers out there.

P.P.S I'm a technical advisor on the Manchester Olympic Committee, which because of our disappointing failure is not the Common Wealth Games Committee, full stop. There you are Roger, sweet as a nut!

Roger – blinkin hell Barry, I'll never get away with all that blagg, she's bound to check it when she sees me.

Barry – Think positive man, you're only after a quick ows yer father, you don't want to marry her, with a few minor adjustments and a lot of vino down her neck you'll be ramming for England.

Liam – Yeah but she's bound to suss his bald head.

Roger – get off you, it's not bald, it's just very fine!

Barry – Come on calm down you two and pass the keg around I'm gagging. Now that's where the few minor adjustments come in, Roger can borrow my old fella's wig for the night.

Roger (shouting) –rubbish man, there's no way I'm wearing a carpet on me bonce!

Barry – Listen, do ya want a bit of skirt or what?

Roger – Yeah well, but...

Barry – There's no buts about it our kid, if it's good enough for Sean Connery, it's good enough for you.

Roger – Alright, I might as well play the game!

Barry – That's the spirit, now Liam go down to the off licence and get 8 cans of Tennants Super, we've got some celebrating to do. Roger's about to feed his pecker with long overdue fruits, and while yer there you might as well post this letter to the lonely hearts, after all the sooner the flood rushes in, the better.

Liam – oh my god Roger, you're gonna have tons of women writing to you.

Narrator – *The scene closes with the lads well pleased at the way things have turned out. For the next fortnight, at least until Roger receives a reply to his letter, life will go on much the same way it always has for them before.*

Act Two

It's one week later and the scene is J.D's Cover-ups, wig-makers and fitters hair salon in Stretford. Where we encounter Eunice for the first time, going about her normal routine with her workmates and the occasional customers. She is adjusting a wig on a rather difficult man's head.

Eunice – Keep your head still darling, I'll get there in the end, don't you worry, it's just a bit of a shrinkage problem, that's all Mr Collins.

Mr Collins – Ah be careful won't you, I've never had this problem before with a refit. Where's it been in the washing machine?

Eunice (laughing) – Oh really Mr Collins you are a card, you know our wigs come from the finest weavers.

Mr Collins – Ow, that's my back you're putting your knee into and do you have to bend my ears down like that?

Eunice – Honestly you're like a little boy with a sore thumb, I'd dread to think what you'd be like if you had to have a baby.

Mr Collins – A bloody freak of nature that's what.

Eunice – If you're going to use that sort of language when ladies are present, you can leave this shop right now and fit this bugger on yourself, there now you've got me swearing against my better nature.

Mr Collins – I'm 'ow' sorry it was just a slip of the tongue, but if I knew it was going to be this painful I'd have taken a dozen aspirins, it's never usually this hard to put on!

Narrator – *As Eunice continues her desperate struggle to fit the wig; her fellow workmate approaches towards her.*

Hazel – Eunice have you seen that wig for little Tommy Stevens, the boy with alopecia, I put it down somewhere and now I can't find it anywhere.

Eunice (shocked) – Er, now you come to mention it, I think I have, is this it?

Narrator – *Eunice quickly whips it off Mr Collins head and hands it over to Hazel.*

Hazel – Thanks deary, I'll see you later!

Mr Collins (angry) – What the hell's going on, I thought this was supposed to be a professional establishment.

Eunice (coyly) – Oh behave yourself and keep your hair on! Oh sorry, I'm forgetting you can't really do that can you?

Mr Collins – How dare you insult me, I'm a valuable customer and I deserve more respect than that, i used to be a lollipop man once.

Eunice – Listen Mr Collins, can't a girl make a genuine mistake now and then without getting her head bit off?

Mr Collins – Yes a girl can; but you're a fully grown woman and you should know better, now go and fetch me my proper hair-piece and be quick about it, I've a very important appointment in half an hour.

Eunice – Oh pardon me for breathing your majesty, yes your majesty, three bags full your majesty.i wonder does a roof thatcher have these problems.

Narrator – *This ongoing commotion draws the attention of Mr James Dawkins, the manger and owner of the wig makers and fitters shop to the drama.*

Mr Dawkins – Now, now, now then Eunice what's going on? The whole shop can hear you!

Eunice – It's him, he's started it, there's just no pleasing some people.

Mr Collins – Well I never, I object most strongly sir to this, the woman's attitude and manner.

I've got a good mind to take my custom elsewhere!

Mr Dawkins – There's no need for that sir, I can assure you, I'll sort this problem out to your satisfaction and it won't cost you an extra penny. Eunice my office at once, now, excuse me Mr Collins, I'll get one of the other girls to see to you right away.

Eunice (crying) – that's right believe his story, boys sticking together and all that; well I'm human as well you know.

Narrator – *Eunice storms off to the office where she is shortly joined by Mr Dawkins.*

Mr Dawkins (lecturing) – I won't stand for that sort of behaviour Eunice, why, if it wasn't for our regular customers like Mr Collins, you and your work colleagues and indeed this shop, would be out of a job and the business would collapse. Do I make myself understood Eunice?

Eunice – Yes Mr Dawkins, But......

Mr Dawkins – But no buts about it, now I'll be keeping a careful eye on you, so be warned. Now, later on this morning, they'll be a young girl from the Y.T.S coming to join our staff and between you and Hazel I want you to show her the ropes so to speak, and remember I want you to set her a good example. Now I'll be going to Leeds in a minute and as you're the senior member of my staff, I'll be expecting you to keep a happy ship. Okay, run along Eunice and no more nonsense.

Eunice – Okay Mr Dawkins it won't happen again, i will be the best pro youve ever had.

Narrator – *Eunice heads off to the ladies room to freshen up, closely followed by her friend Hazel.*

Hazel – Well come on, tell us what happened, the suspense is killing me, has he sacked you or what?

Eunice (lying) – Far from it, in fact I told him that if he ever spoke to me like that again in front of the shop floor, I'd walk out, of course he thought I was bluffing, so I offered him my resignation there and then.

Hazel (shocked) – Oh my god, what did he say?

Eunice – Well let me put it this way, he crawled faster than a crab with mustard up its rear end, telling me, I was too important to the company and he'd always kept an eye on how hard I'd worked for him and without my qualities of trust and leadership, his business would be in a right mess.

Hazel – Are you sure he hadn't been drinking or what, I mean, don't get me wrong Eunice, you're a great laugh to work with, but you don't exactly bust a gut doing much, do you?

Eunice – So are you are you calling me a liar or what?

Hazel – Well it does seem a bit hard to believe!

Eunice – Oh hard to believe is it, well let me tell you something. While I was in his office I told him if he didn't bring in someone to help me and you out in the shop, pronto, like right now, I'd be leaving and guess what?

Hazel – What?

Eunice – He got on the phone to the job centre and its now sorted, a girl will be starting later on this morning and not only that, he's put me in charge today, with a view to one time in the future of taking over the shop.

Hazel – I'll believe that when I see it, anyway we better get back out on the shop floor, Mrs Hamilton has come for her appointment with you, something or other to do with her scalp being tested and I've got Mr Thomas and his blinkin weave to sew.

Eunice – Why do they always come so early? I'm dying for a cuppa and a fag!

Narrator – *Back on the work shop floor of the salon where all the hair raising dramas are played out.*

Eunice – Good morning to you Mrs Hamilton, I hope we're feeling fine today.

Mrs Hamilton – I was until I washed my hair this morning. It's coming out in droves again. The plug hole looked like it had a beard. Oh, I'm so worried, what's going to happen if I go bald, I'm sure my hubby will leave me.

Eunice – Don't you worry about it Mrs Hamilton, its probably nothing, just a bit of stress or something simple like you've been feeling run down recently, most people, especially women see it worse than it is.

Now, if you take your hat off I can take a few hairs from your head and test them in our lab for you, it shouldn't take long, it's just to see what vitamins and minerals you may be lacking. In the meantime while you're waiting I'll fetch you a nice cup of coffee or tea if you prefer, okay, I'll have to have your hat now.

Mrs Hamilton – Oh alright, but promise you won't laugh.

Eunice – Don't you fret Mrs Hamilton, we're all one big happy family here, |I've seen far worse than just a few hairs missing here and there.

Narrator – *Mrs Hamilton removes her hat rather sheepishly.*

Eunice – Jesus Christ! You poor cow, there's not a hair in sight.

Mrs Hamilton (bursts out crying) – What's that you said? I knew you'd make fun of me.

Eunice (apologetically) – Forgive me it was just the shock, I expected to see a lot more hair than that, I promise you we'll do everything we can to help your situation, we have some wonderful treatments here, and should that fail, there's always our state of the art designer wigs.

Mrs Hamilton – it's alright, don't feel bad, at least you're trying to help – not like some people who just make fun.

Eunice – I'll er, just be back in a minute, excuse me, won't be long.

Narrator – *Eunice takes her leave and goes to the office of Mr Dawkins to seek his advice on the matter.*

Mr Dawkins – What is it now Eunice? Can't you see I'm on my way out?

Eunice – Sorry Mr Dawkins, but there's a lady come to have her hair analysed and I've just discovered there's nothing much left to analyse, but a fine downy peach fuzz, what shall I do?

Mr Dawkins – Do the normal procedure in such cases and take a sample from her eyebrows; it will furnish us with the same type of results we're looking for, now really, I must be going, I'm late as it is.

Narrator – *As Eunice and Mr Dawkins leave the office together, Hazel just happens to be passing by close to them.*

Eunice (loud voice) – I hope that girl from the Y.T.S is still coming, I can't do everything whilst I'm left in charge for the day.

Mr Dawkins – Yes, yes Eunice, I promise you she'll be here shortly, so I'm expecting you to keep everything running smoothly.

Narrator – *Mr Dawking's leaves the shop leaving Hazel looking stunned.*

Hazel – I wouldn't have believe it if I hadn't heard it with my own ears. I'm sorry I ever doubted you.

Eunice – Oh you weren't to know Hazel, it's just that I like to keep a low profile; I don't believe in boasting about how important my role is here.

Narrator – *Just then the shop doors opens and in walks Jenny Barlow the young girl from the Y.T.S.*

Jenny – Excuse me, but I've been sent by the Y.T.S and I'm supposed to be starting work here today.

Eunice – Ah yes, we've been expecting you, come with me to the office and while you're filling in the necessary forms, we'll have a little chat about what's what, alright love?

Jenny – Okay!

Eunice – Hazel, when you've finished with your client, can you do me a favour and take some eyebrow samples from Mrs Hamilton and then tell her, we'll send her the results by post with another appointment, meantime if you can try and flog her a wig.

Hazel – I've not got a hundred pairs of hands, you know I can't be in two places at once.

Eunice – Aw, go on Hazel; you can have a long coffee break and read your paper with your feet up when you've finished that, we haven't got any more customers booked in until this afternoon.

Hazel – Oh, alright then, but I'm not making a habit of this.

Eunice – You won't have to again, now that we've got the new girl; come on Jenny love, follow me to my office.

Narrator – *Once in the office, Eunice sits proudly in the managers chair and gets Jenny to fill in her details on the employment form, while she herself, pleasingly surveys her new kingdom, albeit temporarily.*

Eunice – Okay Jenny, when you've finished with the forms, there's just a few questions I'd like to ask you and then I'll show you around the place before we have our elevenses.

Jenny – I've finished filling in the questions.

Eunice – So jenny the first thing is, can you make a good cuppa and have you got a spare ciggie, I seem to have run out of mine.

Jenny – Well, I always make my mum and dad a cup of tea and they think it's very nice, but I'm sorry about the cigarettes, I don't smoke.

Eunice – Oh never mind, one out of two isn't bad I suppose, I'll show you where we keep the coffee maker later.

Jenny – But I don't like coffee, so I don't know how to make it!

Eunice – Well have none of that nonsense here, darling, one of your daily duties will be to make the coffee, otherwise you can sling your hook now.

Jenny – But I thought I was here to learn about, hair and wigs and things like that.

Eunice – You shall, all in good time just like me and Hazel had too, but let me put it like this love, you can't start a car without petrol, that's how important coffee is around here and it wouldn't be a bad idea if you started to smoke as well; we all like to share our cigs here.

Jenny - But I don't want to smoke, it's bad for your health, my dad says it..........

Eunice (cutting her short) – Never mind what your dad says, we'll have no green politics in here clever clogs, now I presume you know how to order things from other shops.

Jenny – Oh yes! I've got a good phone voice and a good memory for ordering new stocks.

Eunice – Good because later I want you to order a pizza with everything on and see what Hazel wants whilst you're at it.

Jenny – But I thought you meant wigs and things.

Eunice (annoyed) – Oh you did did you, well madam, perhaps you'd like to take over my job and run this shop and deal with all its problems and such like. Maybe, getting pizza's is too good for the likes of you.

Jenny – I'm sorry I didn't mean.....

Eunice – Yes, I should think so as well, let's get one thing straight, you're here to fetch and carry and if that means going to the shops for me and Hazel, then that's what you'll do, otherwise you're out, understood?

Jenny (timid and upset) – Yes I understand Miss!

Eunice – Okay now that's more like it, now remain in here while I go and fetch you an overall to work in.

Narrator – *Eunice leaves the office when she meets Hazel*

Hazel – How was she, she looks like a nice girl.

Eunice – Don't you believe it, full of airs and graces that one, still they're all cheeky at that age. Seems to think she can come in here and stroll about, with me and you carrying her, while we do all the work. Give us a ciggie Hazel I'm gasping.

Hazel – Here you are love, looks like you deserve it, the cheeky young mare.

Eunice – Oh you haven't heard the end of it yet, she reckons that she's too good to make coffee for the like of us, but I've smartened her up on that one.

Hazel – I've got a good mind to scratch her eyes out, who does she think she is?

Eunice – Don't worry Hazel, she'll be much nicer now, you'll see, I've brought her down a peg or two. Oh by the way, did Mrs Hamilton buy a wig?

Hazel – She's got to ask her husband first, he's the one with the money.

Eunice – Never mind, stick the coffee on love and we'll put our feet up, I've just got to get an overall for Jenny first. Hey do you fancy a pizza with all the trimmings? My treat!

Hazel – Oh go on then, you've twisted my arm, but I should be watching my figure.

Eunice – Get away with you, you're all skin and bone girl. I'll just get lady muck there to go and fetch them for us; it will give us some time for a gossip.

Hazel – Okay, see you in a minute.

Narrator – *Eunice returns to the office with Jenny's overall*

Eunice – Right, here's your overall, don't put it on yet, I want you to go down to Pizza Hut and get me a couple of big ones with everything on, it's the one on Jepson Street, about 10 mins walk from here!

Jenny – But wouldn't it be better to phone them up and get them to bring it here?

Eunice – Listen love, when you start paying the company phone bills, yes it might, but until that day comes, you'd better do as I say; now off you go.

Narrator - *Jenny does as she's told and quickly leaves the shop, while Eunice returns to the coffee room situated at the back of the salon* *where Hazel is reading the paper and drinking her coffee.*

Eunice – At last a bit of peace and quiet, it's been all go this morning, you'd think the whole world had gone bald.

Hazel –I know what you mean, it's been choc-a-block this blinkin morning.

Eunice – There must be more to life than this, there doesn't seem to be much pleasure in mine.

Hazel – It sounds like you need a man in your life, that will put some spice in your pot my girl.

Eunice – You must be joking they're only after one thing and they'll lie their pants off to get it and then leave as fast as they come.

Hazel – They're not all like that, look at my Alan, they don't come much more loyal.

Eunice – I'm sorry Hazel, no offence intended, but my idea of love isn't a man who sits on his backside all night reading the Daily Sport, farting in between burps.

Hazel – Honestly Eunice, you've got dead cynical lately.

Eunice – Well I wouldn't be like that if there was a decent bloody man out there somewhere for me.

Hazel – So are you telling me, if there was you'd give it a try again?

Eunice – Course I would, I'm pushing 40 now, between me and you I'm getting desperate but I still have my pride.

Hazel – Well kid, check this out, I've just been scanning the lonely hearts column and this bloke sounds right up your street.

Eunice – Go on then read it out but I can't see it making a difference, it's probably some perve after a quick thrill.

Hazel – Okay pin your ears back and listen to this. I'm aged 32 with an athletic build, I'm 5ft 10 inches tall. I've got a flat in Chelsea and one in Manchester; just whilst I'm up here for business and I travel the world a lot, I drive a jaguar and I earn a lot of money, my hair is thick and black and my eyes are gorgeous blue.

I'm an energetic sporty type, please write soon for a date that will be the thrill of a lifetime. P.S. I wouldn't say I was a stud but if I was I would be knocking out winners. Lots of love coming your way you lucky darling Charles. P.P.S. I'm a technical advisor on the Manchester Olympic Committee, which because of our disappointing failure is now the Commonwealth Games Committee.

Eunice – He's got some sauce about him but he's also got that touch of class I'm looking for. Be a darling Hazel and help me write a good letter back, something that's sure to tempt him.

Hazel – Okay, I'll fetch a pen and some paper.

Eunice – Hurry up before floppy drawers comes back from the Pizza Hut, I don't want her knowing.

Hazel – Right here goes, remember I've got to sweeten it up a bit, so bare with me.

Dear Charles, My name is Tanya and I'm 36 years old and single, my eyes are aqua-green and my hair is chestnut. I'm 5ft 10 inches tall and 10 stone, my figure is firm but full and very sexy. I work as a free lance fashion consultant which sees me well paid, I too travel a lot and I own a penthouse in Old Trafford. I love to have fun and lots of it too; if you wish to find out more please ring my phone number written above. Lots of love, Tanya.

Eunice – Talk about tampering with the truth, you know I look more like Alison Moyet and not like the image of Marilyn monroe that you've made me out to be; what's he going to think when he sees me?

Hazel – Listen you're going to arrange to meet him in Conrads Wine Bar in town at 7.30, but being a woman, you're going to turn up an hour later and hopefully, knowing men as I do, he'll be half-pissed by then.

Eunice – But what happens later?

Hazel – Well, by then he will have been won over by your charm and personality, trust me I know what I'm talking about.

Act 3

It's three days later and once more the scene is set in the underground toilets, where Roger and his two work mates Barry and Liam are on duty.

Roger (excitedly) – Lads, it's come, it's come, my dream boat has docked, it's anchored into my harbour.

Liam – Sure you don't mean to say you've got a reply to yer letter at last?

Barry – We were beginning to think all the birds out there had gone frigid or something, I mean that letter I wrote was a real pearler.

Roger – Oh ye of have little faith, I just knew I'd get an answer and here it is.

Barry – Go on then read the bloody thing.

Liam – He's winding us up, yer know what he's like.

Roger – Oh yes, well listen to this boys, if this doesn't get you green with envy, nought will.

Dear Charles, my name is Tanya and I'm 36 years old and single, my eyes are aqua-green.

Liam – What is she, a bleedin fish?

Barry – Shut your GOB and let the man continue.

Roger – Er thank you Barry; where was I? Oh yeah, my hair is chestnut and I'm 5ft 10 inches tall and a round 10 stone. My figure is firm but full and very sexy; I work as a free lance fashion consultant which sees me well paid. I to travel a lot and I own a penthouse in Old Trafford. I love to have fun and lots of it to. If you wish to find out more, ring my number above. Lots of love Tanya.

Liam – Yer jammy bastard, you've hit the jackpot.

Barry – Yeah well done Roger, about time to,. When are you going to ring her?

Barry – Woe a minute, let's think about it, we need a good blag here. First of all, you'll have to put on a posh voice, that really impresses them. Can you do Sean Connery or Roger Moore.

Roger – No but I can do a bit of John Wayne.

Liam – Go on, let's hear it then!

Roger – Get on that damn horse and get the hell out of here, before I milk you both.

Barry – Oh my god Roger that might work on some two bit bag lady drunk on a crate of Meths, but not on a classy piece like his Tanya.

Roger – What am I gonna do, that's the only voice I know apart from my own?

Liam – You could pretend you're a mute and use signals instead.

Roger (not amused) – Ha, Ha, Ha, not funny!

Barry – Come on lads, this is serious stuff we're at the launching pad here, we've got to get her drooling so she comes running.

Liam – Yer not bad with voices and imitating them and all that, why don't yer ring up and pretend yer Roger?

Roger – I've told yer to stop taking the mickey..

Barry – No, hang on a moment Roger, that's not a bad idea, give us the number, I'll ring her now. I think I'll use my Dean Martin, it always goes down well.

Narrator – *Barry rings her number and luckily finds Eunice in her flat.*

Barry – Hello can I speak to Tanya please?

Eunice – Why, who's asking?

Barry – Oh sorry about that, it's Charles, I received your letter this morning and I wondered if you'd like to meet me tonight for a few drinks and some dinner afterwards perhaps?

Eunice – Oh Charles, you do take a lady by surprise, I wasn't expecting you to phone so soon, but yes I'd love to meet you tonight. You can come and pick me up in that big nice car of yours. 7.30 pm will be quite appropriate.

Barry – Er, ah, well about the car, it's been stolen.

Eunice – It's been what?

Barry – Yes, well I don't want to say too much about it, rather distressing and all that. I'm in a business meeting at the moment and it's going to be quite a long one, so how about you meet me at that time in Da Ja Vue Wine Bar on Oxford Road?

Eunice – Oh dear me Charles, I am sorry to hear about the theft of your car, I was really looking forward to a ride in it, never mind I'll meet you at the Wine Bar tonight then.

Barry (evasively) – Oh marvellous, that's a date then, must dash Tanya I'm being summoned to give a lecture now.

Eunice – Okay Charles, see you tonight, bye bye!

Barry – Goodbye my dear!

Narrator – *Barry returns to Roger and Liam with a broad smile on his face.*

Roger – Well, how did it go?

Barry – All the way my son, all the way! She fell for my charm hook line and sinker, i willl score quicker than George best ever did. I'm telling you now she sounds like a right randy goer,well what i mean is, she is up for it.

Roger – What happens now?

Barry – Well, we are gonna close up this place in the afternoon and you're coming home with me for a bit of a spruce up; you've got to look the business tonight.

Liam – What have you got planned for him Barry?

Barry – Well first he's having a bath, then a shave and a loan of one of my Sunday best suits, a borrow of the old fella's hair piece and a pair of my stack heals, believe me the guy will look a million dollars.

Roger – I don't know Barry, it doesn't sound a good idea anymore I'm starting to dump my load now.

Barry – Don't worry, I've got some good Brandy at my yard, you'll soon be raring to go when you've glugged some of that medicine down your throat.

Narrator – *Meanwhile back at Eunice's flat she was in a state of excitement and couldn't help telling Linda (her flat mate) all about it.*

Eunice (excited) – Linda! Linda! I can't believe it; Charles that bloke I wrote to for a blind date, well he's just been on the telephone and he

wants to meet moi tonight, oh I'm dead happy!
Linda – What did he say?

Eunice – Oh it's not what he said, it's the way that he said it, Oh and that voice, real posh like, it reminds me of Frank Sinatra.

Linda – Right lady, get in the bath, tonight you shall be the belle of the ball and I'm going to be your fairy god mother and help you look the part.

Eunice – Oh thanks Linda, I'm dead nervous, it's been so long since I went near a fella proper.

Linda – Don't you worry kid, I'll do your eyes and everything, trust me!

Narrator – *Leaving the girls to their boudoir preparations we find the next scene is at Barry's house, where Barry is with Roger. First he has a bath, then he dresses up in one of Barry's suits and a pair of old stack heels polished off by Barry's dad's hair piece.*

Barry – Wow! You look like a young James Dean, I could fancy you myself; if I wasn't allergic to men, you look so hot tonight matey!

Roger – Listen, just because you work with crap doesn't mean you have to talk it as well.

Barry – I'm not bulling you, I mean what I say, you look like a cool dude from the New York City scene, I mean it Roger that wig is you all over.

Roger (looking in mirror) – Aw rock off Barry, it's got a mad centre parting in it.

Barry – Yeah, but that's all the go with the women now.

Roger – Oh no I don't believe it, just look at my eyebrows their fair and a bit blond.

Barry – So what?

Roger – So what? So what? I'll tell you what, this wigs jet black, that's so what!

Barry – Listen stop being paranoid, the lightings perfect in the wine bar, you could have acne in there and look as smooth and pure as a babys face.

Roger – I'll tell you what Barry, I'm buzzin tonight, when I'm like this I'm god's gift to women.

Barry – That's the spirit Roger, I'm looking for a home run from you tonight, here you are, get some of this brandy down you.

Roger – You bet, I need a boost, are you sure this wig doesn't look like a wig?

Barry – It's a killer mate, I'm telling you. As long as you make sure her hands don't get on yer head, you're on a home banker. Even the centre parting looks the business.

Narrator – *Roger journeys down to the wine bar where the blind date is to take place, meanwhile we return to the flat of Eunice and Linda, where the girls are making last minute preparations.*

Eunice – How do I look Linda? Come on, tell me the truth, I don't want to shame myself, give it to me straight.

Linda – Well if you were a cake you'd be bought every time, you look stunning, that black dress really goes with those shoes and that headbands got your name all over it.

Eunice – Let's hope lover boy thinks the same, with a bit of luck and an arrow thrown my way from cupid himself, I may never have to work again, this Charles sounds my ticket to an easy life.

Linda – Remember Linda, keep him guessing it's the only way with men.

Eunice – I'm a bit worried Linda, what's he gonna say when he finds out I have pink hair and I'm 6ft tall.

Linda – He'll be too drunk to give a damn, because you're going to arrive an hour late.

Anyway kid, it's personality that counts and you've got loads.

Narrator – *So, as Act 3 closes with Eunice leaving her flat to go to the wine bar at 8.30pm and meet Barry, who's also left his friends house to arrive at the wine bar for 8.30pm Both arrive within minutes of each other, half cut and with both eyes scanning the bar in search of their blind date, while they both order drinks at the bar.*

Eunice – I'll have a Black Russian with a slice of lemon and some ice please.

Barman – Right you are darling an Eastern Block special coming up.

Roger – I'll have a pint of the golden amber when you're right mate.

Barman – This is a wine bar sir, we only serve wines.

Roger – Yeah, I knew that, I was just testing you, eh, I'll have some red wine from France.instead.

Barman – Okay sir ,I'll serve you after this lady.

Roger – Sorry love I wasn't takin the piss,I mean mickey or such like, but I didn't see you there..

Eunice – I don't know whether to take that as an insult or a compliment coming from a bloke like you.

Narrator – *As strange as it may seem both were unaware that they were each others respective dates; but it is hardly surprising as their written descriptions of each others appearances are far from the real thing. While they are seated on bar stools watching the door for their expected dates to arrive, they engage in small talk.*

Roger – The music's good in here isn't it?

Eunice – Oh my god, don't tell me I've got to sit here being chatted up by a bar fly. I hate your kind, everything in a skirt is like jam on bread to people like you.

Roger – Believe me, I'm not like that. Call me old fashioned if you like, but I respect women.

Eunice (sarcastic) – Oh well, I must say, aren't you the new man about town, well done for respecting women, how very clever of you.

Roger – Now what have I said wrong?

Eunice – Listen smart arse, if it wasn't for women you wouldn't have a life, so don't talk to me about respect.

Roger – Listen I don't understand what you're going on about but to show there's no hard feelings, I'll fill your glass up, what's your pleasure?

Eunice – A treble Vodka and Orange thank you very much!

Roger (spluttering) – A what?

Eunice – Don't be such a tight-arse you, it's happy hour now, so it won't skin you that much!

Roger – Double Scotch on the rocks and er, a treble Vodka and Orange and give us a couple of bags of cheese and onion crisps.

Barman – Okay sir, coming up.

Roger – Hang on a sec, you better make that plain crisps instead, I'm gonna be doing some French kissing tonight our kid.

Eunice – You're all the same you men, vulgar right down to a molecule, all that is except my Charles, he's a real gent.

Roger – I thought gentlemen didn't keep their women waiting.

Eunice – Listen know all, he's got a really important job – so he's entitled to be a bit late now and again; anyway it looks like you've been stood up.

Roger – Yeah well, it's not only you who can claim to be left waiting because of the other persons job keeps em busy, my Tanya's a busy woman as well.

Narrator – *Suddenly a realisation dawns on them both that perhaps they may be each others blind dates, it must also be known that by now that the drink has played a part in making a weed seem like a flower and a plain person like a real beauty.*

Eunice – Did you say Tanya?

Roger – Yeah that's the girl I'm meeting.

Eunice – Don't tell me your name is Charles?

Roger – Yeah, well it is. Oh hang on a minute ,you don't mean to tell me you're Tanya.

Eunice – The one and only!

Roger – But you said your hair was chestnut, it looks more like salmon to me and another thing you look bigger than you said.

Eunice – You've got a cheek, short-arse, if you're 5foot 10 inches, then I'm king kong and another thing where's this athletic build you described; looks more like a pathetic build to me, oh you lying con artist.

Roger – Listen luv, all the worry of trying to get the Olympic bid for Manchester has stunted my growth and if I'm a bit fatter than I should be ,it's cause of all those functions and eating out I've had to do; what with trying to sweet talk the organisers.

Eunice – Well I only went pink for charity, my normal hair colour is chestnut honestly, mind you at least you've got your own hair, but I can't help thinking it's a style I've seen somewhere.

Roger – Er, yes well, we're here now, so we may as well make the best of it.

Eunice – You don't sound anything like you did on the phone you know.

Roger – I know, it's something to do with air waves, you know, it's like some people are photogenic and others aren't, well I suppose I sound great on the phone, it's that sort of thing.

Eunice – Anyway, we're here to enjoy ourselves and that's the main thing. Oh look my glass is running low and I'm feeling kind of thirsty.

Roger – I like a woman who swings a bit, but Jesus at this rate, I'll be entering you in the Olympic squad for drinking.

Eunice – Well it's a funny thing Charles, cause when I have a drink or two I'm open to any suggestion.

Roger – Barman, bring a bottle of vodka, it'll save time.

Eunice – oh you are a saucey devil Charles!

Roger – Well I like to give a girl a good time!

Eunice (inquisitive) – Tell me something about yourself Charles, I'm fascinated!

Roger – Okay, but I don't like blowing my own trumpet, but if I must, I must. It's like this; Linford Chrstie, Daley Thompson, Torville and

Dean and many many more, they all owe it to me.

Eunice – Torville and Dean, but how come?

Roger – Top secret love, but if I tell you I put the oomph in their engines you'll understand. I'm known in the sporting world as the athletes Winston Churchill. I've just got the gift of inspiring people, if it hadn't been for my bad knees I would have been a champion myself.

Eunice – Aw, I am sorry to hear of your misfortunes, but what happened?

Roger – Well, before I was eighteen, I was as fit as a fiddle, broke all the schoolboy records, running, swimming, tennis, football; you name it ,I was just a natural.

Eunice – But what happened?

Roger – Duty called love, that's what, I saved an old woman's life.

Eunice – But how?

Roger – She was crossing the road and a car swerved round the corner towards her but luckily I was nearby and I clocked it all and I dived full pelt into her path, thus knocking her out of harms way, but sadly to say the impact of the cars wheels shattered my knee caps and thus, end of my career as a fine sportsman.

Eunice – You deserve a saint hood!

Roger – Anyway forget about me, I want to know more about you, but first let's fill the old glasses up barman, get the spirits flowing, same again please.

Barman – Yes sir, quite a big spender aren't you?

Eunice – Well there's not much to know really, except I'm one of the world's leading fashion experts.

Roger – Well give us your marks out of ten for these threads I'm wearin, what d'ya think girl?

Eunice – Well in a formal way your taste is quite quaint and blasé.

Roger – Does that mean I've got it or what?

Eunice – Well I think that might describe you, no I'm only kidding, you're debonair and mature and that's rare these days.

Roger – Listen Tanya, why dont we get something to eat and go to your place?

Eunice – But your swarve flat sounds more cosier.

Roger – Yeah normally it would be, but one of the athletes is staying there tonight with his missus, he's been training hard and not seen her for weeks, so I lent them my flat for a few days.

Eunice – How kind of you Roger, well if you don't mind coming back to a simple girls flat, nothing extravagant mind you, then you're quite welcome.

Roger – No worries, I'm flexible, I'm sure your gaff; I mean flat, is sound.

Narrator – *After a few drinks more they decide to leave for Eunice's flat and by now they're so drunk that they really do start to appear to look like each others descriptions of when they first wrote; such is the wonders of drink, anyway they are now back at Eunice's flat.*

Eunice – Make yourself at home while I open a bottle of Liebraufraumilch.

Roger – What year is it?

Eunice – Does it really matter? Pardon the mood but you get what you see with me.

Roger – D'you know something Tanya, you look exactly as you described, give or take a few inches and the odd bit of pink in your hair.

Eunice – Come to think of it Charles, if you forget the beer belly, you do look like an athlete of sorts.

Roger – I like the flat.

Eunice – Yes it may be quaint but I bet it's not quite as avant-garde as yours?

Roger – Well that's true, it's very different.

Eunice – Charles, I've got a very serious confession, I want to run my fingers through your hair and make mad passionate love to you.

Roger – Well if you forget the hair and make mad passionate love instead, then honey I'm your man.

Eunice – But I want to feel your thick beautiful hair.

Roger – Sorry love it cramps my style having some bird gropping my locks.

Eunice – Oh, so I'm some bird now am I?

Roger – No, of course not, you're special, but so is my hair believe me.

Eunice – Well, at least you're not bald so why should I care?

Roger – Why, don't you like bald men?

Eunice – I've had enough of bald men to last a life time, they're so vain. You'd think once they've lost their hair, they'd be less vain but no way, they get more pickey about a strand out of place, here or there.

Roger – What do you think of syrup wearers?

Eunice – They're the pits, worst of the lot. Hard faced about it as well. Think they can't be sussed but I can spot any man wearing a piece a mile away.

Roger – Oh my god, you can't can you?

Eunice – Course I can, you see, take you for example, you can see that yours is your own, cause you've got a centre parting; no wig wearer in the right mind would ever chance a centre parting; no way.

Roger – Right lets dance, what music have you got?

Eunice – I've got Michael Bolton, Sinead O'conner and David Cassidy; what d'you fancy?

Roger – Well given them choices, how about a big fat pizza? What do you think?

Eunice – Oh you're so funny Charles, come lets cuddle on the sofa first, I'm feeling really sexy!

Roger – Okay, but don't get mad if my hand starts a wonderin.

Eunice – Are you kiddin, I've been saving myself for ages for this moment.

Roger – Okay, how do ya want it?

Eunice – leave off Charles, I'm not some heffer about to give milk, I'm a woman with needs mate, show me some romance will you?

Roger – Okay Tanya, how about this for starters.

Narrator – *The loving couple kiss and hug on the couch in the darkness of the unlighted room, suddenly Eunice grabs hold of Roger's hair or more appropriately his hair-piece.*

Eunice – Jesus Roger, you could do with a good bottle of conditioner on your hair, it's as dry as straw.

Roger – Don't touch it, don't touch it, my hairs too fine to mess about with.

Eunice – I could of swore it moved a bit.

Roger – Don't be stupid, it's a fine Barnett that's all, are you trying to say it's a syrup or what?

Eunice – No, of course I'm not, but it's kinda strange.

Roger – Oh that's right, take the mick out of my mam, I've got her hair or so I'm told its all the rage and dead fashionable.

Eunice – Oh, I'm sorry love, I'm just paranoid, the job I'm in does that. I see wigs day in and day out.

Roger – I thought you said you were a fashion designer?

Eunice – Oh yes I am, but sometimes we come across the odd hair-piece or so.

Roger – Oh, so you're saying I'm bald or what?

Eunice – No of course not, but it does feel different.

Roger – I'm just going to the bathroom, the old dams about to burst.

Eunice – Okay Charles, I'll just slip into something sexy while I'm pouring us both a couple of large ones.

Narrator – *While they are both under the intoxicating effects of alcohol, their visual senses are unaware to such things as their differences, such as size, age and weight.*

Meanwhile Roger is in the bathroom feeling rather paranoid.

Roger (talking to himself) – Oh no, I don't believe it, the wigs slipped a few degrees to the left, it's more like a side parting now, silly bitch, why did she have to touch it? Keep calm, stay cool, I don't think she's sussed it. Look if she had would she be running to her bedroom to yank her kit off. Think positive, you know you're a good looking man our kid, so come on get out there.

Narrator – *Consequently Eunice is in her bedroom wandering what to wear.*

Eunice – I'm sure I had a baby doll nightie somewhere, I bet that cow Linda's took it; never mind, I'll wear my silk gown instead, if that doesn't raise his pole nothing will?

Narrator – *Both join each other again in the living room.*

Eunice – Well big boy, what do you think, it's just a little number I thought I'd slip into. I hope it's to your liking!

Roger – Yeah, it's great, but it would look better hanging up, I'm more your nature man, I like to see the gift not the wrapping paper, know what I mean?

Eunice – Oh Charles, take me in your arms and carry me into the bedroom and make mad passionate wild love to me, I need it, I need it!

Narrator – *Roger tries his best to lift her up!*

Roger – Urhh, Urhh, what the hell have you got in your pockets lead weights or what? Jesus woman, I'm not a fork-lift truck you know.

Eunice – Oh sod it Charles, I'll carry you, It's obvious all your strength is in you know where.

Roger – It's my back luv, it can't take the strain these days; that's the reason I never quite made the Olympics, sods law I suppose.

Narrator – *Eunice lifts up Roger with ease and carries him to the bedroom.*

Eunice – Right I'll go on top; it's my favourite position, it reminds me of when I used to ride the donkey's at Blackpool.

Roger – Yeah and this is one donkey that's gonna make you see the lights.

Eunice – Umm I'm a ridin you cowboy, take me to the moon and back again.

Roger (excited) – Wow, I feel like I've stuck my finger in a plug socket, it's pure electric girl, pure electric.

Eunice – You're suppose to kiss my alps Charles, not lie back with kaleidoscope eyes admiring the view.

Roger – I'm coming! I'm coming!

Eunice – You dare and you're going, you're going, it's only been two minutes.

Roger – Quinta, Paluca, Hava, Teleco, Vinta...

Euncie – What are you saying you?

Roger – I'm trying to name Chile's world cup team of 1962; it's the only way I know that won't let me snow all over your Christmas tree.

Eunice – If that's the case, don't forget the manager and the coaches.

Roger – It's no good stop, stop, we'll have to change positions, I'm getting sea sick with all that bobbing up and down.

Eunice – Oh, I like a bit of variety, it really is the spice of life. Charles you really are creative aren't you; how do you want me?

Roger – Well, if I could have a turn on top, I think I might take you to the heights of heaven.

Eunice – Oh, oh, yeah, yeah, that's it, just how I like it. What's wrong? Why have you stopped?

Roger – What d'you mean why have I stopped aren't you happy with ten minutes or what, most girls only get three. You should thank your lucky stars you've met me.

Eunice – But I've not reached my crescendo yet.

Roger – Ah well, I have and like they say, you pays your price, you takes your chance.

Eunice – Awww, come on Charles, I'm still feeling very sexy, I'll do anything you want, just ask, just ask.

Roger – Okay, I'll have another whiskey and coke.

Eunice – Tell me you're joking Charles.

Roger – Yeah, I'm sorry about that Tanya, I will have my little joke, I meant to say I'll have a triple whiskey and coke.

Eunice – Oh you devil that's right leave a girl unsatisfied, why don't you?

Roger – You're selfish you, I'd see a doctor about it if I was you; it doesn't seem normal to me. I put it all down to greed.

Eunice – But don't you understand a woman's different from a man.

Roger – A likely bloody story, you've been reading too many woman's own magazines; now where's that drink?

Eunice – I might as well of bought a rubber doll for all you've been worth tonight.

Roger – Hang on a minute, I'm feeling sexy again, god you're lucky girl; it must be your birthday.

Eunice – That's more like it, I knew you were only joking, oh Charles you are a tease.

Roger – Ummm that feels nice!

Eunice – Go on, I'm waiting!

Roger – What's wrong with you I'm going ten to the dozen.

Eunice – I can't feel anything.

Narrator – *In the frenzy of lust Roger's wig is knocked clean off his head by Eunice's wandering hands.*

Eunice – Ah! I've scalped you, your hairs gone, oh my god it's gone!

Roger – Oh no what have you done, never mind hair today gone tomorrow.

Eunice (shocked) – You lying pig all the time you've been wearing a carpet on your crown and I didn't know.

Roger – Why was it that good?

Eunice – Never mind was it that good? Look at you, even kojack looks like a hippy compared to you.

Roger – Well, you're no picture yourself are you?

Eunice – Just go, go now, before I call the police.

Roger – Does that mean you don't like me?

Eunice – I'd rather go out with Quasimodo!

Roger – Aw well never mind, at least I broke my duck; it's been ages since I last got my leg over.

Eunice – I'll never speak to another man as long as I live, I feel dirty and rotten.

Roger – I feel great at least I've scored with a great bird even if she does hate me, I'll always have fond memories of you.

Eunice – Do you really think I'm a great bird; that's the nicest thing anyone's said to me in years.

Roger – Yeah, I really mean it, I thought you were great fun. Anyway, I'll get off now, I think I've caused you enough shit, so i will be going.

Eunice – Wait! Don't go, on second thoughts, you look kinda cute with no hair. If it's good enough for Sean Connery, then why not you?

Roger – But aren't you angry?

Eunice – No way, you've got a lot going for you, at least you won't hog my shampoo, or use my hair dryer or clogg my sink.

Roger – Well, if you think I'm that cool I'd really like to see you again.

Eunice – Well I've got a confession to make Charles, I'm not really called Tanya, you see the bald truth of it all is, that I'm called Eunice and I'm a wig makers assistant.

Roger – It's no problem, I can handle that.

Eunice – Oh Charles, you're an understanding angel!

Roger – Well understanding I may be, but Charles I'm not, you see my name is Roger and I'm a toilet technician.

Eunice – Flippin Heck, there's more revelations here than there is in the bible.

Roger – I might not be a brain surgeon Tanya, but if your toilet ever gets blocked up, then I'm your man.

Eunice – I appreciate that Roger and by the way my name is Eunice as I said before, so please don't keep calling me Tanya and if you ever need a wig I'm your girl.

Roger – I think I'll stay natural thanks, I think it's me to be this way.

Eunice – Oh it is Roger, I can't wait for your head to rub against me.

Roger – I'm sorry luv but I had to lie to you about me, otherwise I would never have got a bird here i mean a date.

Eunice – I know what you mean, if I'd have told you I'd have looked like Alison Moyet theres way you'd have turned up.

Roger – Oh I don't know when you're desperate enough, Alison Moyet can easily become Natalie Wood.

Eunice – I know what you mean, it's the same for me, for a moment there, you were my Robert Redford.

Roger – Well I'll be going, I guess it's over now and back to the toilets.

Eunice – Hang on Roger, you might not be Robert Redford, but you're funny and that's better than being mean and alone, please stay, my beds big enough for eight, never mind two.

Roger – Well Eunice, I won't give you an argument about that but you might be in for a shock when the booze wears off and you see me with a sober head in the morning.

Eunice – Are you kidding, I have to see my boat-race every morning, so I'm use to such things, besides, as long as you can kiss and wrap your arms around me who cares.

Roger – Honey believe me I can be your octopus and as for kissing ,well you can call me a sucker any day.

Eunice – Right let's go to bed and this time try to think beyond ten minutes.

Roger – Jesus, you don't want much do you, I could get you a million pound sooner.

Eunice – I'm a girl with a big appetite.

Roger – Holy mother of god this girl wants a marathon not a sprint.

Eunice – You better believe it boy.

Roger – But don't you want to be friends first and lovers next?

Eunice – Turn the light out and I'll answer that question without blinking.

Roger – But I've got to go to work in a few hours.

Eunice – You're not going to work now, I want you to be a bad, bad boy.

Roger – Well I suppose I can take a day off work.

Eunice – Umm, well that's more like it.

Roger – On second thoughts, I'll make it a week!

Narrator – *Like all good stories, the rest is left to the imagination and blind dates can be better than you see.*

The End

www.ingramcontent.com/pod-product-compliance
Ingram Content Group UK Ltd.
Pitfield, Milton Keynes, MK11 3LW, UK
UKHW020237250726
13967UKWH00001B/411